I Will Help You

"Coloured Bedtime StoryBook"

By
Andrea Abbott

Illustrated by
Olivia Villet

ILLUSTRATED & PUBLISHED
BY
E-KİTAP PROJESİ & CHEAPEST BOOKS

www.cheapestboooks.com

 www.facebook.com/EKitapProjesi

ISBN: 978-625-6308-93-0
Copyright, 2024 by e-Kitap Projesi
Istanbul

Categories: Problem Solving, Animals, Family & Friendship
Country of Origin: United States
Cover: © Cheapest Books
License: CC-BY-4.0

For full terms of use and attribution, http://creativecommons.org/licenses/by/4.0/

Contributing: Fathima Kathrada

© **All rights reserved**.

Except for the conditions stated in the License, no part of this book shall be reproduced or transmitted in any form or by any means, electronic or mechanical, including photocopy, recording or by any information or retrieval system, without written permission form the publisher.

About the Book

Mama Heron needs help and Lungile comes to her rescue.

Will Mama Heron be able to help Lungile when he needs help?

I Will Help You
Andrea Abbott
Olivia Villet

"Ouch!" Mama Heron hurts her wing and leg on barbed wire.

"I am hurt. I can't get home to my children."

"Please help me."

"Why are you crying Mama Heron?" "I can't get home to my children."

"I will help you," says Lungile.

"Thank you, Lungile!"

The next day, Gogo sends Lungile to the shop to buy bread.

On the way, he stops to play with his friends in the river.

Eish! The money is gone.

"Don't come home until you find that money!"

"Why are you crying, Lungile?"

"I lost the money Gogo gave me to buy bread. We have no supper now." "I will help you."

Mama Heron's sharp eyes see the coins shining in the water.

"Thank you, Mama Heron."

End of the Story

www.ingramcontent.com/pod-product-compliance
Lightning Source LLC
LaVergne TN
LVHW070454080526
838202LV00035B/2827